# DEAR SERAPHINA

# DEAR SERAPHINA

## A NOVELLA

### AVERY BISHOP

RMS PRESS

# AUTHOR'S NOTE

Epistolary fiction is nothing new—Mary Shelley's *Frankenstein* is told through letters, while Bram Stoker's *Dracula* uses letters, journal entries, newspaper clippings, and telegrams—but it's also something you don't often see. Mainly because it can be difficult to tell a story this way, especially one that's meant to be suspenseful.

Many years ago, working as an editor at a magazine, I had the idea for a story told all in cover letters from a writer sending stories to an editor. Like all writers, this writer wanted to get published, but as the story went on, it became clear that the writer was so obsessed with getting published that it put the editor and his family's life in danger.

(That story, by the way, was called "Persistence.")

With *Dear Seraphina*, I wanted to try something a bit different, telling the story entirely through letters, email, and progress notes. I wanted to play with readers' expectations and emotions, while, at the same time, I wanted to add in a few good twists.

I had a lot of fun writing this novella, and I hope you, dear reader, have a lot of fun reading it.

A.B.

# DEAR SERAPHINA

# PART ONE

Dear Seraphina,

The first movie I saw you in was *Wildcat*. This was a while back, maybe four, five years ago. I didn't see it in the movie theater. Who has the money for that anymore? I certainly don't! But it was playing on TV. I think it was one of those weekends where HBO was free, or some other cable channel had it on. I had worked a long day and was exhausted—I came home and turned on the TV and *Wildcat* was playing. It was already ten minutes or so into the movie by that point. If I'd had the willpower to reach for the remote, I might have changed it.

I don't mean that to come off as nasty or anything, it's just that I was exhausted and, well, it isn't the greatest movie in the world. Though I must admit I'm no film critic. Play me anything that stars Matthew McConaughey, at least the movies where he isn't wearing a shirt, and I'll think it's the greatest thing in the world.

Anyway, I feel like I'm rambling, and I do not want to

ramble, because I know you're a very busy person. I just wanted to let you know that while *Wildcat* is not one of my favorite movies, you stood out. I remember you weren't even the "star" of the movie or anything—your name was like, sixth or seventh once the credits came on—but you were just so . . . *real*. I remember being exhausted from work but sitting up a bit on the couch every time you came on screen. I remember thinking to myself, *That girl sure can act!* Not only that, I remember thinking, *And she is so beautiful!*

How old were you when you filmed the movie? I looked online, but I can't figure out whether you were eighteen or nineteen. I see on IMDb that the movie came out six years ago, and that you recently turned twenty-five (happy belated birthday!), so I guess you were eighteen? Anyway, I feel like I am rambling again, so I just want to add that the very end of the movie, when you walk into the bedroom and find your stepdad dead on the floor and you scream . . . I got chills!

Well, I just wanted to let you know that even though I didn't care much for the movie, I thought you were great in it and have tried watching everything else you've been in since.

Best,

Jennifer Smith

Dear Seraphina,

I realized the other day that, in a way, I'm an actress just like you. Only I don't star in movies and make lots of money. I work as a cashier at a grocery store.

I know, I know, totally glamorous, right? It's an okay job. Sometimes they let me work overtime. I make a little more than minimum wage, but it pays the bills. Or most of the bills. Okay, I am behind on a lot of bills, but that's beside the point.

At least they gave me this rubber mat that I can stand on that helps my back. I guess I'm making it sound like I'm special, but they have the rubber mats for all the cashiers.

Sorry, I realize I'm rambling, just like I did in my last letter. But I wanted to tell you that I realized I'm sort of an actress too. Every day that I clock in, I am playing a part. I smile for all the customers who come into the store. Many of them are pleasant enough, but a few others are . . . jerks.

(I wanted to say something else there instead but thought maybe it was too mean.)

I guess I can't fault them too much. Everyone has their own stuff going on. Everyone is dealing with their own stress, and I'm sure coming into the grocery store for ground beef or canned soup or laundry detergent or whatever is the very last thing they want to do after a long day. And then, you know, they need to stand in line because on the weekdays we don't have every register open, and we only have a handful of the self-checkout registers. So sometimes the lines get long and people get irritated, and they sigh dramatically when they put their items on the conveyor belt, and I have to smile through all of it—just stand there on my rubber mat and smile because my manager is always watching, and if we're not smiling, then the manager makes sure to say something, because "good customer service starts with a smile," which is one of the mottos at the store, and if you get caught not smiling, then you might get written up, and if you get written up enough times . . . oh jeez, it doesn't matter, sorry about that.

But I wanted to say that I am like an actress because every day when I clock in, I have to play a role. I have to smile and make small talk and laugh at the lame jokes some of the older customers tell me when they're paying for their groceries. (You would not believe how many of them still pay with checks!) I don't want to sound too down on it, because many of the older customers are actually very nice and they mean well, but after seven or eight hours standing on that rubber mat, it can be hard to keep smiling, you know? I feel like I am putting on a show, putting on an *act*, and sometimes I wonder if maybe *I* could star in movies too, just like you.

I live only about three hours from Los Angeles. Sometimes I think maybe I could drive up and try out for movies. That's how you get started, right? You have to audition and stuff. I'm sure it's not easy. You probably have to audition for hundreds of things you don't get. But then, once you do get something, once they finally call and say they want you, it gets easier, doesn't it?

Maybe not. Maybe it's all in my head. Because while I do feel like an actress, I know I will never be as good as you. Speaking of which, I watched *She's Not Listening* the other night. So funny! I'm super impressed with your range. You can be in comedies and dramas and thrillers, and I know you have that new superhero movie coming out soon. Is it Marvel or DC? I always get them mixed up. Either way, so impressive!

Well, my hand is starting to cramp up. I'm not used to writing letters by hand like this, and now I've done it twice! Bye for now.

Best,

Jennifer Smith

# FEBRUARY 27

Dear Seraphina,

Seraphina, Seraphina, Seraphina. You have such a pretty name. Did I mention that before? I forget. Maybe I didn't. I don't know.

I wanted to tell you that I went out on a date the other night. It wasn't very exciting. I don't really date much anymore. It's just . . . you know, I don't think I ever told you how old I am. I turned forty-four last month. (Happy belated birthday to me!) There was no celebration or anything. After a while, birthdays don't mean much anymore. They mean a lot when you're young, for sure. I see parents coming into the store all the time to pick up the cakes they special-ordered from the bakery. They get custom messages written on them, in frosting and sprinkles and stuff. Things like "Happy 8th Birthday, Jimmy!" or "Happy Sweet Sixteen, Mary!"

Did you ever do anything fun for your sweet sixteen? I was reading on Wikipedia how you grew up in foster care.

Guess what? I did too. I was taken from my home when I was little. I don't remember much about my parents. By that point, it was just my mom and a guy she was living with. Child Services came in for one reason or another and the next thing I knew, I was staying with other people. They were pretty nice, from what I remember. Gave me my own room and bought me some new clothes. Even gave me an allowance—five dollars a week!—for helping out with chores around the house. But it was a temporary placement, so I started bouncing around to different homes.

To be clear, nothing bad ever happened to me. You hear those horror stories about kids being molested by the foster dads or whoever, and that is all terrible, but I had a pretty good experience for what it's worth. That's not to say I stayed out of trouble. In high school I started drinking and doing drugs and sleeping around. I got knocked up at sixteen and had to give the baby up for adoption, and I'd be lying if I said that sometimes I didn't think about how I had to abandon my child like that. Usually this is late at night when I can't sleep and I've had a couple beers. Oh, yes, I should mention that I still drink, but I don't use drugs anymore. Drugs are bad, just like McGruff the Crime Dog used to say. Or maybe he didn't really talk about drugs so much as just crime in general? Anyway, that was probably way before your time. Like the commercial with the egg and the guy who says, "This is your brain," and then splits the egg open in the pan and says, "This is your brain on drugs." You could probably find that stuff on YouTube if you wanted.

Speaking of YouTube, I watched the trailer for your superhero movie the other day. The little counter on the page said it had 41 million views! That's incredible! I live in a small town of 15,000 people, maybe, and only a fraction come into the grocery store, so I can't even begin to imagine what 41 million people looks like.

Anyway, I'm rambling again, aren't I?

Oh yeah, my date. It was with a guy who works in the stockroom. He's in his fifties and twice divorced. He has kids, I guess, but I don't think he's on good terms with them. If I'm being honest, I had zero interest in going out with him, but I was running low on my food stamps and I hadn't had a hearty meal in a while, so I agreed to go to dinner. That sounds so pathetic, doesn't it? Anyway, we didn't *do* anything, if that's what you're thinking. I was very pleasant during dinner, and then we went to a bar and had some beers and I let him touch me on my hip, but that is basically as far as I let it go.

Well, I'm sure you have better things to do with your time than read about my boring date, so let me just say again that your name is so beautiful. Oh, and that I don't usually go to the movies anymore, but I've started setting aside a few dollars here and there so I can buy a ticket to your superhero movie once it comes out. Only, now that I think about it, maybe I can get the guy from the stockroom to take me. Hmm. Well, take care.

# MARCH 4

Dear Seraphina,

I saw you on the cover of *US Weekly* the other day! You looked so beautiful and commanding, like you *own* the camera. Isn't that what they say?

I was working the morning shift when the woman who swaps out the magazines came in. She is always very pleasant to me, but I get the sense some of the other cashiers don't like her. I guess she isn't nice enough to them or whatever. Don't you think that sometimes people feel too entitled? Like, they expect everybody to be nice to them, but then they don't put in any effort to earn that niceness. Maybe it's just the people I work with. I get along with them okay, though I mostly mind my own business.

Oh, and the stockroom guy? We "broke up," if you want to call it that. I agreed to go out with him again because, well, I thought I could get another meal out of it. And I did! A big bowl of shrimp alfredo and some pretty good garlic bread. And I would be lying if I said I didn't think he was kinda cute. He has a big nose and some of his hair is thinning, but that's okay, I'm not that superficial. And he is actually a really nice guy. At least he is to me. So we went out again and had a nice time at the restaurant, and then we ended up at a bar like last time and had a few beers. I let him put his hand on my hip again, but this time I didn't pull away when his fingers touched the small of my back, or when he leaned in and kissed me on my neck, and then one thing led to another and we were back at his apartment and the lights were off and we were kissing and he was taking my top off and suddenly, I froze.

He asked me what was wrong. I didn't say anything at first—I just straddled him on the couch while the TV was on in the background, some sitcom rerun I think. Then he asked me again what was wrong, and again I didn't say anything, and so he got this weird look on his face and said my name and asked me again. Finally I told him I wasn't sure if we should do this, and he just stared at me for a long time and then nodded and said he understood, and he offered to drive me home. Thank God for gentlemen, right? But, and I know this is going to sound weird, part of me was hoping that he *wouldn't* be a gentleman. We had already got going and there I was on his lap with my shirt off, telling him I didn't want to continue, and I guess part of me wanted him to not take no for an answer. Sick, isn't it?

Maybe I shouldn't have said that. I don't know what I'm saying, just rambling again.

# MARCH 6

Dear Seraphina,

You must think I'm terrible! I hope you won't hold it against me, what I said. Sometimes I think there's something wrong with my head. It's just, well, for some reason I feel comfortable talking to you, like really opening myself up, but then . . . there are some things we need to keep to ourselves, don't we? No matter how much we might trust other people, we always have to keep some secrets to ourselves.

So anyway, I was there on the stockroom guy's lap and basically told him no, but part of me wanted him to force things. Because I am broken, Seraphina. I am sick. I don't think I can ever be in an intimate relationship, not like . . . well, before, when I was with guys I really cared for and even loved.

He was a gentleman, just like I said, and he drove me home. Since then he has not asked me out again, though I did see him in the breakroom the other day and he smiled at me, but that was it. I think he is seeing somebody from the prepared-foods department now. Well, there I go rambling again. I just really needed you to know why I said what I said, and that I'm sorry if it upset you.

I also wanted to let you know again that the *US Weekly* cover really is fantastic. And I read the article inside and it says that you are dating your co-star from *Her Last Move*. He is so handsome! You make such a cute couple. Oh, and I've saved up enough money so I can buy a ticket for the superhero movie. Can't wait!

# APRIL 2

Dear Seraphina,

I heard the awful news that you and your costar from *Her Last Move* broke up and that he is already dating some Instagram model. I am so sorry. Guys can be real jerks! Still, I imagine you can't be that upset, because I read on *Deadline* that your superhero movie made $120 million on its opening weekend! (I know, I know, I sound like such a movie buff, but the truth is I just skim *Deadline* and *The Hollywood Reporter* during my breaks to check up on you.)

And guess what? I did see your movie on opening weekend. I used that money I had saved up to buy a ticket, though I will admit that I went during the matinee because it was cheaper.

But you should know, the whole auditorium was packed, mostly with kids and teenagers and some adults too. I ended up squeezing in between two families down near the front of the theater. And then the lights dimmed and, like, twenty movie trailers played, and then the movie came on.

Oh, Seraphina, it was so good! I had such a great time. That scene near the end, where you jumped from the plane to catch the bad guy? I actually gasped! I know it's all Hollywood special effects, but it looked so real. Later I was looking through IMDb and found that you try to do as many of your own stunts as you can. So I guess I'm wondering . . . *was* that you who jumped from the plane in that scene? Either way, the movie was great.

Bravo!

# APRIL 29

Dear Seraphina,

How are you? I hope you're doing good. It would be nice to get a note back from you one of these days, but I understand you're super busy with all your movie projects. You must get tons of fan mail. Plus, I'm sure everybody is sending you messages on Twitter and Facebook and Instagram and a bunch of other social media places I don't even know about.

Anyway, I heard the good news! That the one and only Steven Spielberg is looking to cast you in his next movie. That is so cool. *E.T.* was my favorite movie growing up. Reese's Pieces were even my favorite candy because of the movie. (Oh Lord, I'm making myself sound so old, aren't I?)

I hope you get the role. I don't even know what the movie is about, but I'm sure you will be great in it.

I did see in the article that another actress is in the running. I forget what her name is. She's the one with red hair. About your age. Petite with a cute smile. She was in that comedy that came out around Christmas, the one with Seth Rogen. Anyway, the article made it sound like Redhead might get the role instead. I really hope that doesn't happen. I mean, she's a good actress from what I can tell, but I still think you'd be so much better in the movie.

So, fingers crossed, Seraphina!

Oh, Seraphina, I'm so disappointed for you! I saw the post on *Deadline* about how Redhead got the part after all. (I know her name now but refuse to use it, because you shouldn't have to think about her anymore.) Anyway, I'm so sorry to hear that, but I'm sure another great role is going to come along any day now.

Dear Seraphina,

Congratulations! I heard the incredible news! I mean, I'm so sorry to hear about what happened to Redhead. The world can be such a crazy place. From what I read, they still don't know who attacked her. Somebody just came out of nowhere and smashed her knee? How awful! And right before she was supposed to start filming the new movie.

But at least you were available, so you could take over.

And now you are going to be in a Steven Spielberg movie! How exciting!

Dear Seraphina,

How goes the filming on the film? (Sorry, that was corny, wasn't it?) I hope everything is going good. I wanted to let you know that me and the stockroom guy went out again. But before you get too excited, let me make it clear that the date . . . did not turn out like I hoped.

I guess the girl he was seeing in the prepared-foods department broke it off, and one day we were in the break-room together and there was this awkward silence, so I asked him how he was doing and he said good, and then there was more of that awkward silence. So I asked him if he wanted to get a drink that night or some other night, and he was quiet for a moment before he smiled and said sure. And so we ended up going out again, back at that same bar, and this time I was the one who made the first move, leaning up on my tiptoes to kiss him on the lips (not sure if I mentioned it before, but he has this bushy beard and it sort of tickles to kiss him), and then eventually we ended up back at his apartment and were on the couch again, and he started to take off my shirt but stopped suddenly and asked if I was sure I wanted to continue. Because, you know, last time I didn't. And I nodded at him and told him that I did want to continue but that I wanted him to . . . be rough.

You should have seen the look on his face. It was like I had just asked him to swallow broken glass. He looked horrified at the thought! I told him that it was okay and that I wanted him to be mean, that I wanted him to hit me, but it was pretty clear right away that he was no longer in the mood. Remember what I said before—"thank God for gentlemen"? Well, in that moment I really wished he *wasn't* a gentleman.

In the end he pushed me off him, but in a gentle way, like he didn't want to hurt me at all, and he tried to stand up. And I had this thought that if I started hurting *him*, then maybe he would start hurting me like I wanted. And so I slapped him, right across the face. He didn't react. He just stared at me. So I slapped him again, and again, and again. And when it became clear that I wasn't going to stop slapping him, he grabbed my wrist and held it tight, and for a second or two I got excited and thought, *Yes, finally*! But he didn't hit me back. He didn't even squeeze my wrist hard. He just forced my hand away from his face and pushed me off him and told me that I should leave. Before, he had driven me home, but this time he didn't even offer that, though he did say he would call me an Uber.

I left immediately and without a word. I felt so embarrassed. I felt so ashamed. I was already thinking about how he would tell the guys he worked with in the stockroom about what happened, and how word would get around the store and I would never be able to show my face there ever again. But . . . well, it's been almost a week now, and nobody has given me any strange looks, at least no stranger than they usually do.

I know you're very busy on set or wherever you might be reading this, so thanks for taking the time. I always feel better after talking to you. I hope the shoot is going great. Tell Steven I say hi!

# AUGUST 18

Dear Seraphina,

Are you still shooting the movie? How's Steven Spielberg? I bet he's real nice. I mean, I know he is obviously super smart and talented, so I just assume that people who are super smart and talented are also nice, but I guess maybe that isn't always the case.

Anyway, I was paging through *People* magazine during my break and saw the news that you recently connected with your biological mom. That's really great. I am so happy for you. I remember reading in that *US Weekly* article a few months ago that you had been trying to track her down. I never got a chance to see my mom again, you know, after I got taken away. Turns out she overdosed when I was like, thirteen or fourteen, and nobody had the heart to tell me. Though sometimes I think I had just been through so many different homes that nobody really knew who my mom was anymore.

It is kinda weird not knowing who your parents are,

isn't it? You grow up around these kids who have parents, who know where they come from, or at the very least still have one parent raising them, but it's their own flesh and blood, a connection to the past. People like us, who grow up not having that connection? We feel lost. Or at least I did. I didn't really fit anywhere. I was always just a guest, staying somewhere temporarily. And I don't know if that's the same for other kids coming up through the system, but even now, despite having my own trailer, a place that has all my stuff (all my "earthly belongings," as the reverend at the church one of my foster families took me to might say), I still don't really think of it as home. It's just a place where I'm staying, like the foster homes growing up, and one day I'll get the word that I need to go someplace else. Maybe that's why I don't have many possessions. Because that way it'll be easier and faster to pack when that day comes.

Well, anyway, I'm happy for you and your mom. Congratulations.

# AUGUST 24

Dear Seraphina,

I was thinking about my letter to you last week and . . . I just want to make sure the woman who says she is your mother really is your mother. Like, have you had a DNA test done?

I'm so happy for you, I really am. The only reason I mention it is I remember seeing something on TV a couple years ago, one of those *Dateline NBC* stories, about someone your age who had been given up for adoption when she was just a baby. For years and years she had been searching for her birth parents, and finally this guy came forward saying he was her dad. He said that her mom had passed away giving birth and he knew he couldn't take care of the baby himself, so he gave her up for adoption. He said not one day had gone by where he didn't regret it and he was now so happy that they were together. A paternity test was done, which confirmed the man was in fact the father, and it seemed like that was it, a happy ending, right?

Wrong.

Turned out the man somehow managed to manipulate the test results. He wasn't really the father. He was just some psycho. And do you know what ended up happening to the young woman? The man locked her in a room so he could rape and torture her and do all these other awful things, and the only reason the man got caught was because a neighbor happened to hear something. The police were called and they searched the house and they found the young woman. The man was arrested and eventually sent to prison.

Seraphina, I just don't want the same thing to happen to you. I mean, I don't think the woman who says she's your mother would do the same awful things that terrible man did, but you're a rich young woman, Seraphina, with a very bright future, and it would be terrible if this woman had come forward just so that she could take advantage of you. I'm going to keep praying for you, Seraphina, because I know one of these days you're going to become such a big star, maybe the biggest in the world, and it would be an awful shame if this woman was playing you so that she could steal all your money.

I saw the interview the other night on TV with you and the woman who says she is your mother. Are you SURE that she's really your mother? Like, have you had the DNA test done, maybe a couple of times, to make sure that there's no manipulation or anything? It is very important you do this. Please. I just want what is best for you.

## SEPTEMBER 16

I've been googling your name every day, Seraphina, sometimes several times a day, and so far I haven't been able to see if you've taken my advice. I do see more and more pictures of you with the woman who says she is your mother. Please, Seraphina, if you do one thing, please take this letter seriously. I can't really explain how I know this, but the woman who says she is your mother? SHE IS NOT YOUR MOTHER.

Dear Seraphina,

It's been a week now, and after seeing all those pictures you post on Instagram, it's clear that you haven't taken my advice to heart, which is very disappointing. I want nothing but the best for you. Do you remember my very first letter? How I told you I watched *Wildcats* one night, and that the movie wasn't so great but that you kept my attention throughout? Do you know why that was, Seraphina? Do you know why I stared at the screen without blinking for nearly a minute before moving off the couch and crawling toward the TV so I could get a closer look? Do you know why every time you came on screen I reached out and touched your face with my finger, so many times that once the movie was over, the screen was covered in my fingerprints?

Inside, I knew. Deep down in that hollow place inside me, the place that opened up when I was forced to give away my baby, I knew. I saw you there on TV—the shape of your nose, the color of your eyes, the way your eyebrows would sometimes raise—and I just knew that you were mine. That you were the baby I was forced to give up.

A mother always knows, Seraphina. She just does.

This entire time I have been wanting to tell you so badly . . . there were even times that I wrote it down, but I knew it was too soon, so I ripped those pages up and flushed them down the toilet. I knew if I didn't destroy them, I might be tempted to send them anyway. So imagine my shock when I saw the article about how you had apparently been reunited with your birth mother. I was devastated, of course. But I was also scared.

For you, Seraphina. I was scared for you. Because I know in my heart and my soul and with every fiber of my being that the woman who claims she is your mother is not truly your mother. I am willing to take a DNA test to prove it. This woman somehow manipulated the test, just like the crazy man from that *Dateline* story.

Please, my sweet daughter, please contact me so that we can finally meet in person and I can give you the hug I've wanted to give since the moment I had no choice but to say goodbye.

Love,

Your Mother

## SEPTEMBER 27

It's been five days, Seraphina. Five days and still no contact. I've included my phone number with every letter I've sent since the beginning. My address too. At the very least, what harm could it do to have me take a DNA test? What do you have to lose?

Do you know what I think? I think the woman who is pretending to be your mother has already put you under her spell. I'm worried that as more time passes, this witch will gain full control. She will take all of your money, Seraphina. Don't you see that by now? That has to be what she wants. I don't care about any of that. You're a talented actress who deserves to be the most famous person in the world, but if you were a nobody just like me, without even a dollar to your name, I would still love you just the same.

Please, Seraphina, call me. You'll hear it in my voice as soon as you do. You will hear the truth.

# OCTOBER 2

I don't understand, Seraphina. It's been a week now since I sent you my last letter, and no phone call or visit or anything. What's worse, I see you posting more pictures with that witch on your Instagram feed! Look, I understand you probably get hundreds, maybe thousands, of letters, and I'm sure some of them are from people who are downright insane and will say anything just to get your attention, but I AM NOT LYING.

Please, Seraphina, don't you understand by now? A mother will do anything for her child, and I've already proven that to you. Remember what happened to Redhead? Yes, Seraphina, that was me. I drove up to Hollywood and followed Redhead around for days, and when I saw the coast was clear, I attacked her. For you, Seraphina. I did that for you! So that you could be in the Steven Spielberg movie! So that your star would rise even higher and faster. I did that for you, Seraphina, because you are my daughter and I love you and I would do anything for you.

But every day that I see you with that WITCH, the more I start to think that you might be an ungrateful daughter after all. That you've become so spoiled that you don't respect your actual birth mother and instead post selfies with that LIAR.

Well guess what, Seraphina—that woman is a FRAUD, and if you don't make things right, I might just have to send my next letter to *Variety* or *The Hollywood Reporter* or *TMZ* to let them know who really hurt Redhead and why.

And I'm not stupid, even though you clearly think I am. I will tell them I did it because you asked me to. That you even paid me to do it. How do you think that's going to go over with Steven Spielberg and the rest of your fancy friends?

I tried to do this the right way, but you left me with no choice. A real mother will go to extreme lengths to do what's right for her child—something this fraud could never understand.

Please, Seraphina, just let me love you . . .

# PART TWO

From: Trent.McAllister@vipprotection.com
To: MikeReynolds@etainmanagement.com
CC: Seraphina Bell's Management Team
Date: October 4, 3:45 p.m.
Subject: Next Steps

**NOTE: This message contains information which may be confidential and/or privileged. It is intended solely for the addressee. If you have received this transmission in error, please notify the sender and delete this message.**

Well, I called it, didn't I?

I told you and the team months ago that I had a weird feeling about this woman. Thank god we didn't pass these letters on to Seraphina. I know she's felt the need to review every single piece of fan mail that comes in, and she would not have reacted well to this.

Mike, as Seraphina's manager, you are certainly the one who makes the final call, but as of right now my advice is to hold off on law enforcement. That would be a PR nightmare. Even a *hint* that Seraphina had any involvement in the attack on Kara Hogan would irrevocably damage her career.

The good news is, over the last few weeks, as these letters became a bit more worrisome, I went ahead and conducted a background check. Most of what we have in these letters is true:

The woman's name is Jennifer Smith. She is forty-four years old. Never married.

She lives by herself in a trailer in Gleason, California, which is about three hours south of LA.

She works at a regional grocery store chain, Weaver Brothers Market, as a cashier, and has worked there for the past five years.

Her credit score is 425. She appears to be drowning in credit card debt.

She did in fact grow up in foster care and does not appear to have any close family ties.

Here's where her account starts to break down though: she actually had two children from two different fathers. There was a girl and a boy, two years apart. When the younger child, the boy, was three years old, he died in an accident. Child Protective Services got involved and took the daughter—then five years old—away. Jennifer was charged with manslaughter, child endangerment, and neglect, but the CPS caseworkers and police made some mistakes in their investigations, and those charges were ultimately dropped. However, Jennifer never got back custody of her daughter. It doesn't appear that she ever tried.

Jennifer has three DUIs on her record, and her driver's license has been revoked. (A copy of the DL is attached, as well as some screenshots from her Facebook page, which doesn't appear to have been updated in over a year.)

I also had our investigators try to dig up that *Dateline*

story Jennifer referenced in one of her letters, about the man manipulating the DNA test. They've reviewed every single *Dateline* episode that ever aired, and that specific story does not appear to exist.

I intend to take care of this ASAP. Due to the sensitive nature of this situation, I am taking on the assignment myself. I will observe Jennifer for two or three days to gauge whether or not she is an actual threat.

If there are no objections from the rest of the team, I will leave for Gleason later this evening and update the team periodically over the next couple of days.

Sincerely,

Trent McAllister

Head of VIP Protection

# PROGRESS NOTE #1

Arrived in Gleason at 10:43 p.m. Behind schedule due to construction on the 405. Stopped by the trailer park first and drove past JS's place: a singlewide with light-blue siding and white shutters. The small lawn out front doesn't look like it's been mowed in weeks. Lights were on inside the trailer. Drove past slowly with passenger-side window down, but couldn't hear anything. Will continue surveillance first thing in the morning.

# PROGRESS NOTE #2

JS's trailer sits at the rear of the trailer park near a cluster of woods. Maybe one hundred trailers total. At 8:00 a.m., I found a place to park across the highway by a gas station. Will remain posted here until she makes an appearance.

# PROGRESS NOTE #3

JS spotted around 9:30 a.m. She wore shorts and a T-shirt and sneakers. Her hair was unkempt. She had on sunglasses. She emerged on foot, pulling a red folding wagon filled with a laundry basket full of dirty clothes. JS continued south down the highway for three quarters of a mile until she came to a laundromat. I parked at a diner across the highway. JS was in the laundromat for approximately two hours before she reemerged. She pulled the wagon with the clean clothes back to the trailer park. I returned to the previous surveillance post.

# PROGRESS NOTE #4

JS appeared again around 2:00 p.m. She wore blue jeans and a dark green polo shirt with the Weaver Brothers Market logo. Her hair was tied in a ponytail. The only item she appeared to have with her was a purse hanging off her shoulder. JS went to the bus stop a quarter mile north of the trailer park. She waited fifteen minutes until a bus arrived. I considered driving straight to Weaver Brothers, which was five miles away, but instead trailed the bus in case she got off at an earlier stop. Twenty minutes later she arrived at the store. She said hello to an older man standing outside retrieving carts. The man smiled in return. She walked in through the entrance doors. Will wait until later to enter the store.

# PROGRESS NOTE #5

Decided to wait until after 5:00 p.m. to enter, as this was a busier time. Spotted JS at one of the registers. She smiled and made small talk with every customer in her line. When she had no customers, she cleaned her workstation and helped bag for the other cashiers.

After a half hour inside, I decided to check out with a few things. I debated waiting in JS's line to interact with her, but before I could, a man in her line raised his voice.

He said: "What do you mean they're not on sale?"

Everybody within earshot paused to look over at JS. The man appeared to be in his mid-thirties, about ten years younger than her.

JS tried to explain something to the man, but he only became angrier.

He said: "I don't give a shit if it's not ringing up. There was a sign there that said they're on sale."

JS glanced past the man toward a manager. The

manager hurried over to speak to the man. Before I could hear the man's reply, another cashier nearby called to me.

She was young, maybe twenty-five years old. She had just turned the light on at her register.

She said: "Sir, I can take you here if you're ready to check out."

I unloaded my cart and watched JS as the cashier rang up the items.

The man was now arguing with the manager: "The sign said they're on sale, but this *bitch* keeps saying they're not."

The manager had previously asked the man to lower his voice, but now she said: "Sir, I am going to ask you not to use that kind of language in here."

This made the man even more irate, and he stormed out of the store.

The manager stepped close to JS, who had started gathering the items the man left behind and setting them aside. The manager asked JS if she wanted to take a break, but she shook her head and said that she was fine. Once the manager stepped away, JS forced a smile at the next customer.

My cashier said: "Is there anything else?"

I paid for my items and returned to my car. I drove across the street and parked at a McDonald's to surveil the grocery store, which closed at 11:00 p.m. JS left the store along with several other employees. JS walked to the nearest bus stop and waited ten minutes until a bus arrived. I followed the bus to the trailer park, where she walked down the lane and back to home.

Will observe her again tomorrow.

# PROGRESS NOTE #6

Despite closing last night, JS had a morning shift today. She took the 7:30 a.m. bus and entered through the front doors at just before 8:00 a.m.

I waited an hour before entering the store. Today I wore a baseball cap and glasses. I picked up pastries at the bakery and then waited in JS's line to pay.

It was quiet in the store and only two registers were open. Like yesterday, JS smiled and made small talk with each of her customers. With me, she noted the pastries.

She said: "Blueberry muffins, my favorite."

I paid for my items and went straight to the trailer park.

I drove past JS's trailer. In the daylight, it looked even more rundown.

I made note of the other trailers nearby. None looked occupied.

The rear of the trailer park is woodland. A quick GPS search on my phone showed a shopping mall on the other side of the woods, approximately a quarter mile away.

I drove to the shopping mall and parked near the edge and slipped through the trees. It took me less than ten minutes to come up on JS's trailer from behind.

All of the windows were closed, locked, and shaded by curtains. The rear patio sliding door was locked with a wooden dowel rod on the bottom track.

I walked around to the front of the trailer. The lane was still deserted. Now wearing latex gloves, I picked the lock on the front door and entered.

The trailer had a distinct odor of cigarette smoke. An ashtray was on the coffee table, as well as two empty packs of Pall Malls. The living area was mildly cluttered with books and magazines and mail. I noticed a few past due notices and several issues of *US Weekly*.

In the kitchen area I found several empty beer and rum bottles in the trash. The fridge was sparse, but there were six bottles of beer inside.

On the counter was a grocery list. Comparing a photo of one of the Seraphina letters to the grocery list, it appears that the handwriting is a match.

I found a legal tablet in a drawer. Some pages had been ripped off, and the yellow coloring of the paper, as well as the dark blue lines, match the paper of the letters mailed to Seraphina.

Under the mattress on the floor in the bedroom, I found several pictures of Seraphina torn out of magazines. In every picture, her eyes had been scratched out.

A few of the pictures also included Seraphina's mother.

In those pictures, her mother's entire face had been cut out from the pages.

I returned the photos to where I found them and exited through the rear patio sliding door. I propped up the wooden dowel rod against the side of the door so that it would fall in place once the door was closed. I returned to my car in the shopping mall to type up this note.

JS may be less stable than she appears to be on the surface. Uncertain of next steps. Will continue to observe.

# PROGRESS NOTE #7

Something curious happened.

I was sitting in the McDonald's across the highway from Weaver Brothers Market at a table in the back. The time was 2:55 p.m.

I heard a voice behind me: "Mr. Beef Jerky and Barbecue Potato Chips."

I turned to find the young cashier from yesterday. She wore the store-branded polo shirt, but there was no nametag. She held a McDonald's bag, and it appeared she was ready to leave.

She apologized and told me she always noted certain items in people's purchases, and that was how she remembered them: Mr. Beef Jerky and Barbecue Potato Chips. Miss Low-Fat Greek Yogurt and Evian Water.

Then she said: "Oh god, maybe I'm wrong. You were in the store yesterday, weren't you?"

I told her that I was.

She said: "That's right. You were there when that jerk was yelling at Jenny."

I realized I had a potential opening here. I picked up my phone, discretely hit "Record Memo," and then set the phone face down on the table so the cashier couldn't see.

I asked: "Was she okay?"

The cashier said: "Who, Jenny? Yeah, she was fine. A bit rattled, I guess. But we have jerks like that come in all the time. Some are just louder than others."

I said that JS had appeared calm while the man was yelling at her.

The cashier said: "Yeah, well, Jenny's been working at the store for years now. She knows the drill. When a customer gets like that, you just smile and wait for a manager to intervene."

I said that I had noticed the manager offer JS a break, but that she had declined.

"That's Jenny for you," the cashier said. "Takes everything in stride."

Then she glanced down at her watch, ready to leave. I realized I was about to lose my chance, and scrambled to come up with something to say.

I asked: "How long have you lived in Gleason?"

The cashier gave me a weird look, and I did my best to explain. I told her that I recently went through an ugly divorce and transferred to a position in my company down here. I mentioned how I hadn't even had a chance to unpack all of my stuff yet.

The cashier said: "I'm sorry to hear that."

I said: "I hate to admit it, but being new in town can be sort of overwhelming. Kind of like being a fish out of water. I guess I was wondering if you had any good recommendations for, well, anything in this town. Restaurants, bars, whatever."

The cashier thought about it for a moment.

"Honestly," she said, "there isn't all that much to recommend in this town. Except Weaver Brothers, I guess."

She grinned when she added this last part, and I smiled, trying to think how I could bring it back around to JS.

I asked: "So no good bars in the area? No place you and your coworkers like to go to unwind? Especially, you know, after dealing with jerk customers like that guy from yesterday."

The cashier shrugged and said: "Yeah, it can be stressful. I guess maybe that's why Jenny drinks so much. Heck, one time she got so wasted I drove her home from the bar so that she didn't leave with some creep."

The cashier named some bars in the area and then checked her watch again before saying she had to go.

I watched her get into her car—an older model Toyota Corolla—and exit the parking lot to drive across the highway to the grocery store. She parked on the side, what was evidently the employee lot, and went inside the store.

Observation: Consistent with her three DUIs, it appears JS is still a heavy drinker. Perhaps she wrote her letters while she was drunk.

From: MikeReynolds@etainmanagement.com
To: Seraphina Bell's Management Team
Date: October 7, 2:30 p.m.
Subject: Urgent – Read ASAP

**NOTE: This message contains information which may be confidential and/or privileged. It is intended solely for the addressee. If you have received this transmission in error, please notify the sender and delete this message.**

By now I'm sure you've all heard the news. Somehow it leaked to *TMZ*, and we're still trying to figure out how and from whom.

Seraphina called me less than an hour ago, demanding answers, and I explained to her that I wasn't sure what happened. I assured her that as soon as we know more, she will be informed. I also stressed that it was imperative she tell anyone who asks that she has no idea why Trent McAllister would have been in Gleason, California, let alone in that trailer park.

I must stress this again to the team: *Seraphina must have full deniability*.

Here is what we know thus far:

Trent's last progress note came in at 5:30 p.m. yesterday. When I didn't hear anything by 11:00 p.m., I texted him and received confirmation that he was continuing the surveillance. That was the last I heard.

This morning I received a heads-up from a contact at *TMZ* minutes before the story went live: Trent's body was found in Jennifer Smith's trailer. He had been stabbed multiple times in the chest. (My contact, by the way, has no idea who leaked the story, though he suspects it came in via the tips section of their website.)

Police had received an anonymous complaint of a disturbance. When they arrived at the trailer around 1:30 a.m., they found Jennifer passed out on her bed. She still had the knife in her hand. When awakened, she appeared disoriented. She denied having stabbed Trent. She did admit to meeting him at a bar, though she stated she did not remember leaving with him. She was placed under arrest and transported to the nearest detention facility to await arraignment.

I've been in touch with a law enforcement contact who reached out to the current investigators in Gleason. He claims the police found no evidence inside the trailer that links Jennifer Smith to Seraphina. I told him that we believed there were items under the mattress, but he insisted the police did a thorough search and found nothing. When asked about a notepad, he said that some papers were found in the trailer, but not the paper tablet I had described.

My suspicion is that Trent was trying to cause an escalation which would warrant a petition for psychiatric hospitalization; this was something he had mentioned to me privately before he left for Gleason, an idea he wasn't quite prepared to share with the rest of the team. He may have provoked Jennifer Smith to the point where she stabbed him to death. Though knowing Trent and how professionally he's handled challenges in the past, it's hard to believe he would have allowed things to progress so far— that he'd provoke Jennifer to the extent that she would have grabbed a weapon. My contact stated that Trent did not have any defensive wounds on his hands or arms.

As I'm sure you all now know, the *TMZ* article goes into great detail about how Trent had been accused by multiple women of sexual assault over the years, though none of the charges ever stuck. Still, it is true that this ultimately drove him into early retirement from the police force and led him to start his own security firm. We have to consider the possibility that Jennifer Smith acted in self-defense. In any case, it is imperative that Seraphina's name comes nowhere near this. At least, no closer than it already has. The *TMZ* article notes that Trent and his company work exclusively with Seraphina, which, let's be honest, is the only reason *TMZ* is covering the story in the first place. (And now, of course, it's being picked up by every trade magazine and tabloid in the country.)

All of the letters from Jennifer Smith have been shredded and burned. Trent's correspondences had been sent via encrypted email, so we should be good there.

Everyone must delete those messages, as well as this one, immediately after reading. As far as we know and as far as the media is concerned, he acted alone.

Mike Reynolds

Senior VP of Etainmanagement

# PART THREE

# OCTOBER 18

Dear Seraphina,

By now I'm sure you've heard the news. Everyone has. How Trent McAllister tried to drug and rape yet another victim. How before he even had a chance to unbuckle his belt, he was stabbed to death.

You're probably asking yourself what kind of person takes another person's life. Even if it is in self-defense, killing another living, breathing soul isn't an easy thing to do. There is a moment before the tip of the knife pierces flesh when you ask yourself if you really want to take this next step. And then, before you know it, the moment passes, and there is no turning back.

I want to tell you why I did what I did. I want to try to make you understand.

I wasn't lying when I said that you and I are much the same.

We both grew up in foster care.

We both grew up wanting to act.

Of course, you reached your dream. You've starred in major Hollywood movies. You're famous and beloved around the world. You have a team that works with you closely—a team that will obviously do whatever it takes to protect you.

Me, I played small roles in high school plays and later at a local theater, but I've never managed to break into the movies, or even TV, like you have. Don't get me wrong, I've tried countless times, but nothing ever worked out in my favor.

I suppose if I had kept at it—beating the pavement for auditions, so to speak—I may have gotten lucky eventually. Because that's usually what it takes, right? Talent and determination, absolutely, but a little bit of luck too. Being the right actor at the right audition at the right time of day with the right casting director . . . it's like a line of cosmic dominos, perfectly aligned and falling at the perfect moment. I could imagine turning on the TV one day and pointing out to my friends: "Hey, look, that's me!"

Then again, it's not like I have any friends. That's one of those things left over from foster care. As you know, Seraphina, growing up in the system can be tough. It's hard to make friends. It's hard to open yourself up to people when you know they might leave you for a different home at any time.

You never did receive any of my letters, did you? Part of me had thought that might be the case. So when you saw the news about Trent McAllister and what had happened to him, the name Jennifer Smith meant nothing to you.

I want to tell you so much more about me, Seraphina, but I'm not sure how to do it. It might be easiest if you put yourself in my shoes. That shouldn't be too difficult, with all your acting experience, and since we both had a similar upbringing.

So imagine, if you will:

Growing up, you don't have a mom or a dad to take care of you. Instead, you're forced into the foster care system. Overall, the experience is positive—the homes you're placed in are nice enough, the foster parents decent people—but you understand from a young age that you can't really be yourself. You have to smile even when you're sad, because if you don't, questions are asked, so many questions, and then you're sent to see a psychologist, who asks even more questions.

The only way to navigate the foster care system, you come to realize, is to act.

And as time goes by, you find that you actually enjoy playing a role. You enjoy acting. And so in middle school and high school, that's just what you do. But while you know your acting skills are good—you play Rebecca Gibbs in *Our Town* and Ann Putnam in *The Crucible*—those skills are nowhere near as good as you wish they could be.

Professional training is out of the question—far too expensive—but you do your best with what you've got, and after high school, you save up enough money to move to Los Angeles.

After two years, you've gone on countless auditions,

and while there have been a few nibbles, there are never any bites.

You have a few friends that you've gotten to know, fellow aspiring actors who you've met around town. You and your friends go out drinking at night. And you find that the less luck you have on auditions, the more you end up drinking, and the more you drink, the easier it is to forget.

This is how you meet Trent McAllister.

Though *meet* might be too generous a word. You are a girl at the bar. He is a guy at the bar. He's a bit older than you typically like, but he's cute enough that when he offers to buy you a drink, you say yes. And, well, you don't know what happens after that.

Much of that night is a blur. Except for the part where the two of you end up in some motel room. You're only partly conscious by that point. You are aware that you're naked, and that you're face down on the mattress, and that a man is on top of you. You try to speak. Tell him to stop, to get off you. But he doesn't. In fact, it seems the more you protest, the more aggressive he becomes. And he is brutal. Like he wants to punish you for something beyond your control. It doesn't matter how much you beg, how much you cry, he won't stop.

Until finally he does. By that point, all the fight has drained out of you. You just lie there on the bed, bruised and broken, barely aware when he goes to the bathroom to wash himself off and get dressed.

As he opens the door to leave, this stranger from the

bar—the one whose cheeks grew dimples every time he laughed at one of your silly jokes—tilts his head slightly and says, "Thanks for the good time."

Later—much later, once you've begun to heal—you wonder about all the ways things could have been different. All the ways you could have prevented what happened. Whether or not there had been any warning signs from the start.

You don't know who the man is. He never gave you his name. But you're sure you would recognize him if you ever saw him again. His eyes—those piercing blue eyes—still haunting you.

You start going out more, almost every night. But you don't go out to have a good time. You go out to find him.

You love to act, and that's exactly what you do—you play the role of just another young woman at the bar, drinking and dancing and having a good time. Guys buy you drinks, and you act like you drink those drinks, but you only take a sip or two before you dump them out when the guys aren't looking.

You need to stay alert. You need to keep an eye out, so that when he shows up again, you're ready.

A few months later, you spot him.

He's already selected a victim. She looks to be about your age, blonde with a tight black dress. She's with friends, but it's clear they aren't *close* friends. Just like you on the night you were selected. He no doubt knew close friends wouldn't let one of their own go home with some random guy, at least not without getting some information first, just in case. The guy is smart. He knows how to pick them.

You watch him flirt with the blonde. She's already tipsy, throwing her head back every time she laughs. When he offers to buy her a drink, she says yes, and after he pushes through the throng of people to the bar and raises a hand to flag the bartender, you edge closer.

Just as you suspected—as he turns away from the bar, he surreptitiously drops a pill into the girl's beer. He shakes the bottle slightly to dissolve the pill as he makes his way back to the girl, and when he hands her the drink, she leans forward and kisses him on the cheek.

Your stomach drops. You want to rush over there and knock the beer from the girl's hand. But the truth is, you had been expecting this. That's why you've been prowling all these bars and clubs the past couple of months. Waiting for him to show up. Waiting for him to select another victim.

You're prepared. You know what needs to happen next.

Pretty soon, the pill takes effect. The girl starts to stumble a bit. She appears loopy. And the man, expecting this, holds her closer, the dimples in his cheeks growing larger as he laughs like she's just said something funny.

He makes sure to scan the club one final time before he directs the girl toward the exit. He is big and strong and manages to lead her along with no problem, right past the bouncers at the door and into the night.

You follow the sound of her Jimmy Choos clicking hollowly off the sidewalk. Down one block, then another.

He gets her into his car, slumped over in the passenger seat, and then hurries around to slide in behind the wheel.

As soon as he's in motion, you hurry to your own car and speed down the street to catch up with them.

They end up at a motel fifteen minutes away. The man doesn't stop at the front desk to get a room; apparently he's already secured one. He helps the girl out of the car and straight to a door on the first floor.

Again, your stomach drops. The motel room you eventually exited—after crying on that soiled mattress for what felt like hours, afraid to walk through the door into a world that would forever now look and feel and smell different to you—was on the first floor too. Getting up a flight of stairs with a half-conscious girl isn't easy. The man knows what he's doing.

But what sickens you even more is the fact you don't immediately call the police—you have to wait. If he isn't caught in the act, they might not be able to charge him. So you need to wait; despite how much it tears you up inside, you sit and wait. After ten agonizing minutes, you finally make an anonymous call.

You park across the street at another motel. You slump low in your seat when the police cruiser arrives ten minutes later. Two cops get out and look around the parking lot before they slowly approach the room number you reported. One of them knocks on the door while the other stares out at the street.

After a minute, the door opens. The man is standing

there. It looks like he hurriedly put on his shirt and is busy tucking it into his pants.

For a second or two, he looks apprehensive.

And then a smile splits his face.

He steps out of the room and closes the door behind him. He shakes the first cop's hand, then shakes the second cop's hand. They talk for a minute, and during that time the man's expression hardens, and he starts scanning the area, clearly searching for the person who called in the tip.

You slump even lower behind the steering wheel. For a moment it feels like the man's gaze has zeroed in on you, those piercing blue eyes penetrating your soul. But as one of the cops continues to talk, the man finally nods and then goes back to the door. He opens it but doesn't step inside, just holds the door open long enough for both cops to glance in. One of the cops grins at the man, slaps him on the back, and then they return to their cruiser as the man shuts the door and hurries to his car.

You don't move for the longest time. Even when your legs start to cramp up. You just hide behind the wheel, staring at the motel, not knowing what to do next.

The man must be a cop. That much is obvious based on the familiarity of his interaction with the two officers. And now that you think about it, he even *looks* like a cop. Tall and broad-shouldered with a steel jaw and a clean crewcut.

You didn't plan for this. You consider calling the motel directly, or even crossing the street and demanding to speak to the manager in person. But that won't work. The manager won't tell you anything. Besides, it's doubtful the man—the cop—gave his real name or paid with a credit card.

In the end, you leave.

The girl, you tell yourself, will be fine. She will eventually make it out of that motel room, just like you did so many months ago. She might not be the same girl anymore, but at least she will survive.

You scribbled down the man's license plate while you followed them, and the next day you look him up. His name is Trent McAllister, and he is indeed a cop. You do more research, scouring local news articles and diving deep into social media. You learn that over the past several years, two women have come forward alleging sexual assault, but in the end neither of the charges stuck. Trent remains an active police officer.

With no other recourse, you contact the *Los Angeles Times*.

You speak to a reporter about your experience. She is an investigative journalist who stays on the story for weeks, surveilling Trent McAllister much like you did, but in the end, she admits that she doesn't have enough to publish an article. But she does threaten the police chief that she will do so, bringing up your story and how you witnessed what took place that night with the blonde, how two officers showed up but did nothing. One thing leads to another and soon Trent McAllister is pushed out of the force.

But men like Trent McAllister always end up on their feet. There are no formal charges he has to reckon with. He walks away scot-free, with a sizable pension, from what you're told. He gets into the private security business, looking after B- and C-list celebrities who can afford him on the cheap, until eventually he is hired to protect one of Hollywood's rising stars.

As for your next steps, you decide to leave Los Angeles. You end up in a small town three hours away. Get a job as a cashier at a grocery store. Decide to put your past behind you.

Then one day at work, you see him again.

It's a rainy weekday morning and not very busy, only a handful of customers trickling in and out of the store. The woman who comes in to swap out the magazines in their little racks on the front end is by your register. You make small talk with her, paging through the most recent issue of *OK! Magazine,* when suddenly your heart stops.

The woman notices the sudden silence and looks up.

"What's wrong?" she asks.

You don't respond. You just continue to stand there, frozen, staring down at the open page. There's a shot of a young actress standing on the red carpet of some premiere. The actress looks gorgeous in her Versace gown, smiling with her hand raised to wave to the crowd. But it's the man standing just behind the actress that has caught your eye. He's barely in focus, but it's more than enough to recognize him.

Trent McAllister.

And just like that, you're back in that motel room, naked and pressed face down into the bed.

"Hey," the woman says, gently touching your arm. "Are you okay? You look pale."

Without a word you pivot away, straight to the bathroom. You need some time alone. Some time to think.

In the bathroom stall, you get out your phone and google Trent McAllister. It doesn't take long to learn that he created his own company, VIP Protection, and that he had been hired to provide security to the young, beautiful actress.

Almost immediately, you start to form a plan.

Trent McAllister deserves to be punished for what he has done. Not just to you, but to all the women he's raped.

And so you begin to write letters to that young, beautiful actress. Letters that start out innocuous enough, but whose tone, over time, begins to escalate. After all, you have to take it to a place where Trent McAllister will feel the need to get involved.

Now, if you have one regret, it's what happens to Kara Hogan. You need to prove your devotion to the young, beautiful actress. To show Trent what you're capable of. There is simply no other way to do it.

Once you send your last few letters, you know Trent will show up sooner or later.

And he does show up, exactly as expected.

Part of you worries that he'll recognize you from that night so long ago, that the plan you've so carefully constructed will fall apart like a house of cards.

But when he does look at you, he barely even blinks.

Getting him in the trailer the next night isn't difficult.

Stabbing him once he's in the trailer, well, that turns out not to be difficult either.

And slipping the knife into Jennifer Smith's hand as she lays unconscious on her bed?

Easy as pie.

---

Kids go into foster care for many different reasons. From what I've read, Seraphina, you were abandoned as a baby. Your mom had you when she was very young, and she was scared and didn't know what to do, so she left you outside the hospital one night with a note saying she hoped you went to a good family. Immediately afterward she regretted it, but she knew she would get in trouble for abandoning you like she did, so she didn't come forward. But that didn't stop her from always thinking about you, and eventually tracking you down so many years later.

That wasn't the case for me or my brother. While I don't remember much about him anymore, I do remember that I loved him more than anything else, and when he died, it was like my whole world had been ripped away from me.

Our mother didn't care much for either of us. We were an inconvenience. A burden.

When my brother and I cried, our mother yelled at us, which made us cry more, which made her yell more. An emotionally abusive cycle. She would leave us by ourselves, which meant there was a five-year-old looking after a three-year-old for hours at a time.

One day, when our mother wasn't home, my brother and I were sitting in front of the TV. When I left to use the bathroom, my brother decided to do what he'd been trying to do ever since he was able to stand up on his two chubby feet: climb up onto the kitchen counter.

As soon as I realized he'd left his spot on the carpet, I called out his name. I heard a noise and hurried into the kitchen. And there he was, standing on the counter. I screamed. The panic in my voice caused him to whip his head around, which caused him to lose his balance, which then . . .

I'll never forget what happened. Even now, after all these years, I can close my eyes and see him falling. It's like it all happened in slow motion. The surprise on his face from hearing me scream. His eyes widen. His mouth opens. And then he falls. Head first.

I was frozen. I wanted to rush forward, wanted to catch him, but I couldn't move. I couldn't breathe. All I could do was stand there and watch him fall.

As soon as I heard him hit the floor, I snapped out of my paralysis. I rushed forward, already feeling tears on my face. I kept saying my brother's name, but he didn't respond.

I knew that in the event of an emergency, I should dial 911. But we didn't have a phone.

I ran out of the apartment. Since it was a weekday, I

had to knock on six or seven doors until someone finally answered.

An ambulance was called. So were the police. And then Child Protective Services.

I never saw my brother again.

I was placed into the custody of CPS. I started my journey through the foster care system, but the girl who had been taken from that apartment—the one who had stood frozen in place while she watched her brother fall to his death—was different now.

As I mentioned before, Seraphina, I learned to play a role. I learned to *act*.

And, well, years later, after my time in Los Angeles, I decided to confront the woman who had once been my mother. During those years in LA, I had tracked her down —I'd had no interest in seeing her, even though she lived only a few hours away; I was just curious about where she ended up. But now, with nowhere else to go, feeling alone and directionless, I decided to confront her. If not for me, I told myself, then for my brother.

That was how I ended up in Gleason. Not to live there. Certainly not to settle down there. But simply to confront the woman who I hated most in the world.

I found a hotel to spend the night, with the intention of going into the store the next day. I hoped she'd be working. I would go to her line. I would look her in the eye. And the moment she recognized me—because what mother wouldn't recognize her own child, even if twenty years had passed?—I would tell her just how much I hated her.

But guess what, Seraphina? She didn't bat an eye. She smiled at me like I was any other customer that happened to pick her register. She even made small talk, though for the life of me I can't remember what she said. I was too shocked by the fact that she didn't recognize me. She didn't even pause to look at me again, as if she thought she might know me from somewhere.

I don't know why, but it was like Trent McAllister had drugged me and taken me to that motel room all over again —only this time it was my soul that was bruised and beaten.

I left the store in a kind of daze. I wondered if maybe I had made a mistake. If the thin woman at the second register with the long dark hair and sharp cheekbones and a bit too much makeup wasn't actually Jennifer Smith.

But her nametag said JENNY. And she looked exactly like I remembered her. She was two decades older now, yes, but you don't forget your own mother.

I wasn't sure what to do next. I could try to face her again, but what good was confronting her if she didn't know who I was?

Then inspiration struck. I still had some money left. So I got an apartment. I applied for a job at the grocery store, and pretty soon I was working shifts as a cashier.

Jenny, as everyone in the store called her, actually trained me. It was a surreal feeling, standing behind the register scanning strangers' items while the woman who had given birth to me stood a few feet away, coaching me on what to do if a customer presented a check or a bill of more than twenty dollars or an expired coupon that they insisted I must accept.

I worked there for several months. I became friendly with much of the staff. I learned that Jenny had worked at Weaver Brothers for years. That she wasn't married and that she didn't have children, or if she did, she never talked about them.

Jenny still went out drinking, sometimes with people from work and sometimes by herself. She had several DUIs under her belt and no longer had her driver's license, so she took the bus everywhere. There were a few bars near the trailer park, and she often ended up at one of those late at night.

One night I'd gone out to the bar just to observe her. Jenny got wasted. A seedy-looking guy started talking to her. It was clear he planned to take her out of there and that she was in no position to make any decisions on her own, and I had a flashback of that night at the club when Trent McAllister left with the blonde in the tight black dress.

I still felt guilty for not helping that woman, so I decided to intervene.

When the seedy-looking guy asked who I thought I was, I said I was her daughter.

If Jenny heard this, she barely reacted, practically passed out on her feet, and soon I had her in my car and took her home.

When I pulled up in front of her trailer, Jenny seemed to wake up a little. With her head tilted back on the headrest and her eyes closed, she smiled and said, "Did you tell that guy you were my daughter?" Then, the smile fading, her voice went low and quiet, almost plaintive: "I had a daughter once. A son too."

I managed to get her into the trailer. I'd needed to fish the key from her purse to let us in, and I didn't realize I had forgotten to return it until I'd laid her down on the mattress and then returned to my car.

I ended up giving Jenny back the key the next day at work; I said I found it on the floor in the breakroom, that she must've dropped it. I didn't tell her how I'd gone to the hardware store earlier that morning to have a copy made. Even then I couldn't say why I had done so, only that deep in my gut, I felt I might need it someday.

Why did I end up staying in Gleason? Well, Seraphina, I liked the place. It was nice and quiet. The people at work were good and decent, and I enjoyed what I did. As I said in one of my letters, every day was like a new acting experience. I put on a mask for the customers, became a different person. Especially when I was around Jenny.

Then one day I opened a tabloid magazine and saw you —and standing behind you, Trent McAllister.

As soon as I learned about his connection to you, an idea began to form.

You see, Seraphina, I realized that it wasn't just Trent who needed to be punished, but Jennifer Smith too. For being a terrible mother. For what had happened to my brother.

She never faced any jail time, by the way. It's true what

Trent McAllister had written in his notes: there had been some kind of screw up on the police's end, which resulted in the charges being dropped. She had lost her son, and she had lost her daughter, but she never wanted either of us in the first place, so that wasn't much of a punishment, now was it?

After a couple of weeks, that inkling of an idea still hadn't grown into anything substantial. How, I wondered, could I do something that might bring Trent McAllister and Jennifer Smith together? The question haunted me— so much so that one night I woke up suddenly, as if from a nightmare, except instead I was exhilarated by a revelation.

That inkling of an idea had finally grown into something. It had rooted into my brain, spawned branches and leaves.

I still had the copy of Jenny's key. On one of my days off, I snuck into her trailer. I looked everywhere to find stuff that had her writing on it. Scraps for a grocery list, anything. Eventually I found enough of what I needed, just the right amount that would give me the chance to practice her handwriting. And once I did that, I started sending you those letters—letters, I knew, which would eventually pique Trent McAllister's interest.

I'd needed to set a trap, and the fictional version of Jennifer Smith—the one that wanted to be abused during sex—was the bait.

I figured Trent wouldn't send a lackey to take care of this situation—he'd want to do it himself. But I didn't know when. Every day after sending that last letter, I kept glancing toward the entrance doors, expecting the next customer to walk through to be him.

When he eventually did come, pushing one of those small shopping carts like any regular customer, I felt my heart stop again. Suddenly I wasn't sure I could go through with it. Especially when he finally came to check out. I had to step away from my register. I felt like I had all those years ago, five years old and watching my brother fall to his death.

The asshole yelling at Jenny is what finally broke my paralysis. I stepped back on the rubber mat, turned on the light to signal that my lane was open, and asked Trent McAllister if he was ready to check out.

I can't begin to describe to you how difficult the experience of facing that monster was for me. It felt like every muscle in my body had tensed up. I realized after maybe thirty seconds that I'd been holding my breath and I was worried he might notice, but he was busy watching the scene two checkout lanes over.

In the end, Trent barely even glanced at me. Even if he did—even if he had taken a long look—I wasn't worried. It had been almost two years since I'd met him at the club. I had dyed my hair since then. Cut it short too. And even if everything was the same as it had been that night, I doubted Trent would have noticed. He hadn't seen me as a person at all, but as his prey.

As soon as I finished the transaction and handed him his receipt, I knew he would want to get inside Jenny's trailer to see her things, if he hadn't done so already.

I'd been anticipating this. For months, I'd been cutting out pictures of you from magazines. I'd scratched out your eyes for dramatic effect. With the pictures of your mother, I'd torn out her entire face.

As soon as Jenny had left for work the next morning, I'd used the key to let myself in. I hid the pictures under the mattress on the floor. I put the yellow legal pad—the one I'd used to write all my letters to you—in the kitchen.

Then I left and waited in my car at the end of the lane so I wouldn't be noticed. Eventually Trent McAllister showed up. He entered the trailer and was in there for some time. As soon as he was gone, I went back inside to retrieve everything I had planted.

I followed Trent for the rest of the day. It wasn't difficult. When he entered the McDonald's across the highway from the grocery store, I went in too, wearing my work polo, like I was heading to the store, even though I actually had the day off. I bought a Big Mac and fries to go, and once everything was bagged, I approached Trent at his table.

I came up with some silly reason to talk to him, but he seemed to buy it. Especially when I mentioned the incident the previous day, where the customer was yelling at Jenny. That certainly got his attention. I could tell he wanted to ask more, but I knew telling him too much, at least right away, might raise a red flag. After some back and forth, I finally managed to tell him exactly what I wanted him to hear, except . . . well, there's a funny thing about that.

You see, much later that night I went through Trent's

phone. I read the encrypted messages he sent out to your team. I was curious if he would mention our interaction, and he had, but he left out one particular detail.

"Yeah, it can be stressful," I'd said. "I guess maybe that's why Jenny drinks so much. Heck, one time she got so wasted I drove her home from the bar so that she didn't leave with some creep. When she gets enough alcohol in her, she'll go home with anybody."

Do you see what Trent did there? He omitted that last part.

For the rest of that afternoon and early evening, Trent stayed parked at the gas station across the highway from the trailer park. He only moved after Jenny walked up the lane to the highway. She had changed into a low-cut blouse and tight jeans with heels. I remembered the night I drove her home, and I figured she smelled of cigarettes and that same cheap perfume.

She walked to one of the bars nearby, a real dive, and went inside. By that time it was almost ten o'clock.

Trent waited until eleven o'clock before he entered the bar.

And what happened after that? Well, one can only imagine, especially if they'd seen how Trent treated the blonde in the tight black dress back in LA. I didn't bother going inside. I waited out in a parking lot across the highway. Almost an hour passed before Trent came back out of the bar, guiding Jenny toward his car as she drunkenly stumbled on her heels.

As soon as Trent got her into his car and pulled out

onto the highway, I started my car. But I was in no hurry. Unlike last time, I knew exactly where they were headed.

Trent pulled into the trailer park a few minutes later.

I parked in the shopping mall behind the woods, put on a pair of latex gloves, and then hurried through the trees, coming out behind Jenny's trailer. I had the copy of her door key in one hand, and in my other hand was something I'd taken from her trailer earlier that day.

I paused at the rear of the trailer, tried to listen to what was happening inside. I couldn't hear anything besides the TV.

I hurried around to the front, looking around to make sure there were no witnesses. Then I went straight to the front door, unlocked it, and stepped inside.

Trent had just gotten started. He'd pushed Jenny down onto the mattress and was in the process of yanking off her jeans. He didn't hear me until the last moment, when I'd stepped on a part of the floor that creaked. He stood up straight and spun around, and that's when I plunged Jenny's kitchen knife into his chest.

How many times did I stab him, Seraphina? I honestly can't say. So far every article I've read online has noted "multiple stab wounds," but there has not been an official number released.

I knew it would take more than just one stab to end his life. I would need to do it twice, maybe three times. But once I started, Seraphina, I couldn't stop. All I could think about was what he had done to me in that motel room, and what he had done to that blonde in the black dress, and to all the other women who had come before us and after us, and I stabbed him for each and every one.

He fell to the floor. He didn't move. He didn't breathe. He just lay there, bleeding out onto the carpet.

I stepped back, the knife still in my hand, and looked over at Jenny. She was passed out on the bed.

I edged around Trent McAllister's body and crouched down next to her. For a moment, I thought she might open her eyes—her lids fluttered briefly—but they remained closed.

Putting the knife in her hand, I pressed down hard to leave her fingerprints.

I stood to leave, but then considered Trent McAllister again. I knelt beside him and searched his pockets, taking out his iPhone. It was a newer model and could only be accessed by passcode or Face ID. All I needed to do was point it at Trent's face—his eyes were still open—and then I was in.

After I read through everything, I returned the phone to his pocket.

Before I left, I pulled the disposable phone I'd purchased weeks ago from my own pocket and called 911.

On the way home, I tossed the trailer key and pieces of the disposable phone down several different sewer grates.

I couldn't sleep at all that night, Seraphina. Not one wink. I was too wired. I kept refreshing the browser on my laptop, waiting for the moment the local news website updated.

By nine o'clock that morning, it had.

Not much detail was given—they didn't list any names, of course—but the short article noted there had been a fatal stabbing at the trailer park and police were still investigating.

I copied the URL, went to TMZ.com, and clicked on the button that asked "Got a Tip?"

Oh yes, I had quite a tip indeed.

Hours later, *TMZ* ran the story. They reported that Trent McAllister, whose company worked exclusively for you, had been found dead in a trailer in Gleason, California. They noted that not many details had been shared by the police, but that several women had accused Trent of sexual assault during his time as a police officer.

It hasn't even been two weeks since the incident. Jennifer Smith has been charged, of course. A good defense lawyer could make the case that she had simply been trying to protect herself from a rapist. But that wouldn't explain *all* the stab wounds. She will probably face some time in prison.

My brother deserves a whole lot better, but at least it's something.

And me? Well, yesterday I put in my notice at the store. I told the managers that I'd enjoyed working there, but that it's time to move on. One of them asked where I planned to go, and I smiled and said Los Angeles.

That's right, Seraphina, I'm headed back. After all this time playing a role (the role of a lifetime, some might say), I realized my acting skills have improved significantly. So I figure now's a better time than any to start auditioning again.

I know, I know. Acting can be a tough gig. But at least I no longer have any reason to be afraid of the city. I know that if anybody tries to hurt me like Trent McAllister hurt me, I can handle them.

And I know it's not going to happen overnight, getting my first role. It's going to take time. It's going to take talent and determination. And a little bit of luck, of course.

Maybe one of these days, Seraphina, you and I will meet on set. We might pass each other, and I might smile at you and you might smile back, and maybe that will be the end of it. Or maybe I'll have a scene with you. We'll talk off camera. Share some stories and jokes. Become friendly with one another. Maybe even become real friends.

And maybe one of these days, Seraphina, I'll share this letter with you. Probably not—although I may be a risk taker, I'm not stupid—but I do like the idea of one day telling my story to someone, and if I share it with anyone, I figure it might as well be you.

I imagine you'll be dumbstruck at first, once you read all these pages. I won't blame you; it's a lot to take in. You might be furious at Mike Reynolds, assuming you haven't already fired him. You might even try to make amends with Kara Hogan, put her in one of your movies, do what you can to advance her career. Because you're that kind of person, Seraphina. You're *good*.

Me? I wouldn't call myself good. I wouldn't call myself

bad, either. I guess if I had to call myself anything, I'd call myself a survivor.

After some time, when you've managed to process this letter and everything I've been through, you'll tell me that you understand I had no other choice. You might even hug me. Tell me that it's over now. And of course, I'll hug you back. I'll thank you for understanding.

I've never had any real friends, but I think you could be my first. After all, we are much the same, you and I.

So until that day, Seraphina, I wish you well.

Yours truly,

A Fan

# ABOUT THE AUTHOR

Avery Bishop, whose books include *Girl Gone Mad* and *One Year Gone*, is the pseudonym for a *USA Today* bestselling author of more than a dozen novels.